Sheltie
the Shetland Pony

Written and illustrated by **Peter Clover**

ALADDIN PAPERBACKS

New York   London   Toronto   Sydney   Singapore

For Stephen and Missy

First Aladdin Paperbacks edition May 2000

Copyright © 1996 by Working Partners, Limited
First published 1996 by Penguin Books Limited U.K.
Created by Working Partners, Limited

ALADDIN PAPERBACKS
An imprint of Simon & Schuster
Children's Publishing Division
1230 Avenue of the Americas
New York, NY 10020

Library of Congress Cataloging-in-Publication Data
Clover, Peter.
Sheltie the Shetland pony / written and illustrated by
Peter Clover. — 1st Aladdin Paperbacks ed.
p.   cm. — (Sheltie ; #1)
Summary: Emma is dubious about moving to the country until she meets
Sheltie, a very clever Shetland pony who solves the mystery of who is
stealing a neighbor's cabbages.
ISBN 0-689-83574-4 (pbk.)
[1. Shetland pony—Fiction. 2. Mystery and detective stories.] I. Title.
PZ7.C62475Sm   2000
[Fic]—dc21   99-87893

Chapter One

"I wish we didn't have to move to a new house," said Emma. "And I wish we didn't have to go and live in the rotten countryside either!"

Dad raised an eyebrow behind his newspaper. Mom smiled and scraped butter on to a piece of toast for little Joshua.

"I bet everyone will be horrible," moaned Emma. She poured some milk into her cereal bowl. "Why do we have to move anyway? It's nice here!"

Mom gave Emma a stern, no-nonsense look.

"Because Daddy has a new job. And besides, it will be nice for you and your little brother to grow up with fresh air to breathe, and green fields to run and play in. You'll love it, Emma. Really you will. Just wait until you get there. It will be a new start for all of us. A real adventure. You'll simply love it."

"I won't," Emma muttered. She stuck out her bottom lip and made her face look even more unhappy. "I'll hate it! I know I will."

By lunchtime, everything was packed up and ready to go. It was a long drive to Little Applewood and it was almost dark by the time they arrived. It was too late to see or do anything, so they all went to bed early.

The next morning, Emma woke to a strange crowing sound.

What is that? Emma wondered, still half asleep. She rubbed her eyes and blinked at the unfamiliar surroundings.

Outside, the rooster crowed again. Emma decided to investigate. She slipped out of bed and peered through the window of the funny little attic room that was her new bedroom.

It was a glorious, sunny day. Emma could see green hills rolling far off into the distance, with cows and sheep grazing in the meadows. She saw a little stream, winding its way through an orchard of old apple trees. She saw a field of golden corn and a smaller field with a fence around it.

Then Emma's eyes grew wide. Inside the fence was a fat little Shetland pony. A very small horse, no taller than Emma herself. It looked like a giant guinea pig.

The pony was light chestnut-colored, and it was resting its fuzzy chin on the top bar of the wooden fence.

Emma got dressed and rushed downstairs. She couldn't find her shoes anywhere. There were boxes and packing cases all over the floor in every room. Finally Emma found her old sneakers and put them on at the back door. Then she raced out into the yard.

A little path ran from the house right down to the fence. When the pony caught sight of Emma, it dashed around in a big circle.

Emma stood up on the bottom rung of the fence, resting her arms over the top bar. The pony trotted over to say hello. He pushed his soft, velvety muzzle into her hands.

"What a nice face you have," said Emma. The pony's brown eyes twinkled beneath his bushy mane.

Emma stroked his head and pushed her face closer for a better look. The pony seemed to be smiling. Emma threw her arms around his neck and snuggled in with a big hug. The pony just stood there as quiet as a lamb.

"I see you've already met Sheltie," called Mom, crossing the yard with a handful of fresh carrots. Emma spun around, jumping off the fence.

"He's beautiful. Who does he belong to?" asked Emma.

Sheltie saw the carrots and sprinted across the field at lightning speed.

"He's yours if you want him to be," said Mom, knowing already that Emma did. She fed Sheltie a carrot. The carrot disappeared in a flash.

"Sheltie belongs to Mrs. Linney, who sold us the cottage," said Mom. "But she can't keep him in her new city apartment, so he can stay here and live with us. Would you like that, Emma? Your very own pony."

"Oh, yes," said Emma excitedly. "I'd like that very much."

Mom passed Sheltie a carrot and Emma laughed as it disappeared as quickly as the first.

"Will I be able to ride him?" asked Emma.

"Of course," said Mom. "He's just your size. And Mrs. Linney is coming over this afternoon with Sheltie's tack. She's going to give you your very first riding lesson and tell you how to look after him."

Chapter Two

Mrs. Linney wasn't at all like Emma had imagined. She wasn't six feet tall and as thin as a pole. She was short and squidgy and round, like a dumpling. She wore scruffy clothes and old sneakers like Emma's.

Emma sat on the fence and watched Mrs. Linney come plodding up the front path with a saddle and bridle slung over her arm. A tiny black riding hat for Emma sat perched on top of her head.

"Hello there! You must be Emma."

Emma smiled. Then Sheltie nudged her in the small of her back and gently knocked her off the fence.

"Ow!" Emma laughed, and Sheltie shook his head, blowing and snorting. His eyes twinkled, full of fun and mischief.

Mrs. Linney plopped the saddle over the top of the fence and ruffled Sheltie's long, shaggy mane. Sheltie grabbed one of the buttons on Mrs. Linney's cardigan between his teeth. He tried to pull her into the field, through the bars of the fence. Emma giggled.

"He's a real terror, isn't he, Emma?" Mrs. Linney pulled the cardigan free.

Sheltie spat out the button onto the grass at her feet.

"You're going to have your hands full with this one," said Mrs. Linney, handing Sheltie a treat. "You love your peppermints, don't you, Sheltie?" Sheltie's eyes sparkled.

Mom came out to watch as Mrs. Linney saddled up Sheltie. He had short legs and a huge stomach that almost brushed the long grass. It was funny watching the leather girth being strapped around his fat belly. Sheltie kept nipping at Mrs. Linney's bottom with his teeth every time she bent over, and tugging at her tweed skirt.

Mrs. Linney was all smiles. "Now then. Let's get you up, Emma. You're not nervous, are you?"

"No," said Emma. She was really, just a

tiny bit, but she wasn't going to say anything. All the same, it felt very odd sitting
up in the saddle on Sheltie's back. He was
only a Shetland pony, but it seemed to
Emma that she was a long way from the
ground.

Mrs. Linney showed Emma how to hold

the reins, and how to position her feet in the stirrups.

"Toes up, heels down."

Emma laughed and sat with a straight back and elbows tucked in, hands low.

"Perfect. A proper little horsewoman," said Mrs. Linney. That pleased Emma.

"Now, all we're going to do today is to walk on, nice and steady, with me holding the leading rein. We'll walk around the paddock, this small, fenced-in field. Ready?"

"Hold on a minute," called Dad, striding from the house with a camera. "Say cheese."

Emma grinned. Sheltie grinned too, or at least he appeared to. He really did have a funny, smiley look about him.

Mrs. Linney led Sheltie around the paddock in a gentle circle. Sheltie was on his best behavior. Emma's grin spread until the corners of her mouth almost touched her ears.

"Way to go, Emma," said Mom, clapping her hands. Mrs. Linney walked alongside as Emma and Sheltie circled the paddock.

"Am I good?" asked Emma.

"You're wonderful," said Mrs. Linney.

Emma leaned forward to pat Sheltie's hairy neck. "You're the best pony in the whole world," she whispered in his ear.

"There's no doubt about it," said Mom. "Those two are going to be the very best of friends."

"Walk on," called Emma. "Walk on."

Chapter Three

After Emma's riding lesson, Mrs. Linney came into the house for a cup of tea. They all sat at the kitchen table as Mom passed around the cookies.

"Always remember to bolt the gate properly," said Mrs. Linney, "otherwise Sheltie will open it. He's a very clever pony."

At that moment, Sheltie trotted right in

through the open kitchen door. He skidded across the floor tiles with a clatter of hooves. He went straight for the table and lunged at the sugar bowl, sending the milk carton flying. Mrs. Linney fell off her chair with a bump.

Before anyone could stop him, Sheltie

was crunching a mouthful of sugar cubes.

"Sheltie, you naughty boy!" Mrs. Linney pulled herself to her feet.

"Always remember to bolt the gate properly," said Mom with a laugh. Emma giggled.

"Come on, Sheltie." Mrs. Linney led the way outside. "As you can see, Sheltie's a very determined pony. There's not much he can't do. Opening gates is his specialty."

They took Sheltie back outside. Mrs. Linney showed Emma how to lock the gate properly, and how to fit the little pin in place to prevent Sheltie from sliding the bolt across.

Sheltie was frisky, and watched all this with great interest.

At the far end of the field was a little shelter made of stone. It looked like a little house.

"This is Sheltie's field shelter," said Mrs. Linney.

Emma rushed inside. Sheltie followed, looking very pleased with himself. Inside, on the back wall, was a feeding trough.

"This is for Sheltie's pony mix. One small scoop a day. And this rack is for Sheltie's hay."

Outside, Mrs. Linney showed Emma how to fill the water trough from a rubber hose fixed to the wall. Sheltie stuck his head in the trough and blew bubbles. Then he tried to drink the water straight from the hose. Emma got soaked, but she didn't mind.

"There's plenty of grass in the field for Sheltie to graze," said Mrs. Linney. "So you only need to feed him once a day." Sheltie shook his head from side to side, whipping both of his cheeks with his long mane.

Emma thought having a pony of her very own to look after was going to be great fun. Living in the country wasn't so bad after all.

Every evening, when Emma said good-night, Sheltie would follow her to the gate and watch her walk through the yard to the house. And the very first thing Emma did each morning when she woke was to look out from her bedroom window to see Sheltie standing by the fence, waiting for her with a twinkle in his eye.

Sheltie was Emma's very best friend.

✪ ✪ ✪

It wasn't long before Emma could ride all by herself.

One day, Mrs. Linney came over and led Sheltie and Emma down to the end of the road at the side of the house.

Halfway down the road, behind a stone wall, sat another house. This house's garden wasn't filled with flowers like Emma's garden. It was a vegetable garden.

Sitting up in the saddle, Emma could see right over the wall. She saw rows and rows of cabbages planted in neat, straight lines. She saw tomatoes and green feathery carrot tops sprouting from the freshly dug earth. She saw onions, too, and corn, all planted out beautifully in carefully arranged rows.

As Sheltie and Emma passed by, an old man's head popped up from behind the wall.

"Good morning, Mr. Crock," said Mrs. Linney.

"Bahh!" grunted the old man. Then he ducked down again, behind the wall.

Emma turned her head right around and stared at the man.

"Don't take any notice of him, Emma," smiled Mrs. Linney. "He's just an old grump who cares about nothing but his precious vegetables." Sheltie stuck his nose up in the air and plodded on.

At the end of the road they turned around.

"Okay then," said Mrs. Linney. "Off you go." Emma was going to ride back down the road to the field, all on her own.

Emma was a bit nervous, but proud and excited at the same time. She patted Sheltie's neck, then squeezed with her heels.

"Keep walking, Sheltie, keep walking."

Sheltie was very good. He walked at a slow pace down the road. He seemed to know that Emma's first ride was very special.

Sheltie was on his best behavior . . . until they came back to Mr. Crock's vegetable garden!

Chapter Four

Suddenly, Sheltie stopped. Emma kicked her heels, but Sheltie just stood there, peering over the wall into Mr. Crock's vegetable garden.

"Keep walking, Sheltie. Keep walking," called Emma. But Sheltie just rested his head on the stone wall. His nostrils twitched as he smelled the fresh carrot tops and cabbages.

Mr. Crock popped up again from behind the wall, all angry and grumpy.

"Go away!" he snapped. "Go on, get out of here. And keep that filthy pony away from my vegetables."

Emma's heart thumped in her chest. "Keep walking, Sheltie! Keep walking."

"Scram!" yelled Mr. Crock, and Sheltie flew. Emma held on tight, as Sheltie bolted all the way back to the field. When they got to the gate, Sheltie slowed down to a walk.

"Great job," called Mom. Little Joshua waved and clapped his hands.

Sheltie trotted over, looking for a treat.

"There was a mean man," said Emma. "He called Sheltie a filthy pony."

"Just ignore him," said Mrs. Linney, coming up behind her. "He's just a grumpy old man. Just because the summer fair is only two weeks away, he thinks everyone is after his prizewinning vegetables."

"I don't want his rotten old vegetables," said Emma.

"No," smiled Mom, "but he probably thinks Sheltie does."

"But you don't, do you, Sheltie?"

Of course, Sheltie said nothing. But there was a mischievous look in his eyes. And Emma was sure that all Sheltie could think of were those juicy carrots and cabbages.

The next day, it rained. Dark clouds filled the sky and it poured and poured. Sheltie didn't mind the rain, but Emma couldn't ride him that morning. Instead,

Mom drove Emma into town to buy her new school clothes.

"Yuck!" said Emma. She wasn't looking forward to starting her new school. She wanted to stay at home with Sheltie.

Emma sat in the front seat of the car next to Mom. Little Joshua sat in the back, strapped safely into his car seat. Sheltie watched the car glide down the road and out of sight. He gave a loud snort and shook the rain from his shaggy mane. Then he stamped his hooves. Sheltie wanted to go with Emma. He looked around the empty paddock, then trotted over to the gate. He began to think of those juicy carrots and cabbages in Mr. Crock's Vegetable garden.

Sheltie stood at the gate and looked

down at the bolt. He had watched Emma open and close it many times. First Sheltie nudged it with his muzzle, but nothing happened. Then he took the little pin between his teeth and pulled. The rest was easy. Sheltie pushed the bolt across and nudged open the gate.

Sheltie felt very pleased with himself and gave a loud snort. The rain stopped and the sun began to shine as Sheltie trotted up the road, splashing through the puddles.

Mr. Crock was busy in the garden shed. He didn't see Sheltie push open the gate. Sheltie looked up and down the neat rows of vegetables and sniffed the air. The vegetables smelled good.

Sheltie put his head down and pulled a huge carrot out of the damp earth. The carrot was very juicy and very crunchy. Sheltie thought it tasted delicious. Then he tried a cabbage. That was good, too.

Sheltie was eating his second cabbage when Mr. Crock came out of the potting shed. Mr. Crock's face turned to thunder when he saw Sheltie standing in the middle of his precious vegetables.

"Scram!" he yelled at the top of his

voice. Sheltie jumped, and ran away as fast as he could. He tore through the gate and back down the road to his paddock.

Emma's dad was in the kitchen, pouring himself a cup of tea. Mr. Crock burst in through the back door hollering and shouting.

"That animal of yours has been in my garden, stealing my cabbages." Mr. Crock sounded furious. "I won't stand for it," he said. "If you don't keep that pony away from my vegetables, I'll call the police and have them take him away!" Then, before Dad could say a word, Mr. Crock stormed off in a huff.

Chapter Five

When Emma came home, Sheltie was hiding in his field shelter. Dad had fitted the paddock gate with a padlock and chain. He told Emma what had happened and said that the paddock gate must be kept locked at all times. He showed Emma how to use the padlock and the key. Poor Sheltie was in disgrace.

"What a lot of fuss over a few cabbages," said Mom. But Sheltie had been naughty, and it was wrong of him to steal Mr. Crock's vegetables.

The next day, Mom baked a nice apple pie, and Emma wrote an apology to Mr. Crock in her best handwriting. Together they took the pie and the letter along to grumpy old Mr. Crock.

Mr. Crock wasn't pleased to see them. But he took the apple pie all the same and grunted when Emma handed him the apology.

"Just keep that pony out of my garden," said Mr. Crock. "I don't like ponies. And I don't like them eating my cabbages. Like I said before, if I catch him again, I'll call the police and have them take him away."

Then he stomped off into his shed.

Emma bit her bottom lip and was close to tears.

"Can Mr. Crock really make the police take Sheltie away?" asked Emma.

"I don't think so," said Mom. "But we'll keep an eye on him all the same."

Emma was very worried. All day long she kept rushing to the paddock gate to check the padlock and make sure it was locked. It always was.

Emma wore the key around her neck on a piece of string. Sheltie was very frisky. He thought this was a new game and kept trotting over to the gate to nibble at the new lock and chain.

Two days later, Mr. Crock arrived at Emma's cottage with a policeman. There was a sharp knock at the door. Mr. Crock stood in the doorway. Emma's mom looked surprised. Dad looked puzzled.

"That pony of yours has been eating my cabbages again," said Mr. Crock. "I warned you what would happen if you didn't keep him out of my garden." His face looked angry and mean. "That pony is a thief!"

The policeman gave Emma a polite smile. He couldn't believe Mr. Crock was making all this fuss over a few vegetables.

"But that's impossible!" cried Emma. "Sheltie's gate is locked and I have the key right here." She dangled the key from the piece of string for the policeman to see.

"Well, miss, two more cabbages have gone missing. And Mr. Crock here says it must be your pony."

They all went outside and down to Sheltie's paddock. The chain and padlock were firmly in place, and the gate was locked and bolted. Just as Emma had left it.

The policeman walked around the paddock looking for any broken fencing. Sheltie followed the policeman, tossing his head. He thought this was another new game.

"Well, Mr. Crock," said the policeman, "there doesn't seem to be any way that this pony could have possibly escaped. I'm afraid there is nothing I can do." The policeman smiled and gave Emma a pat on the head.

"What about all the hoof prints, then?" said Mr. Crock. "That proves it, doesn't it? Come and take a look." They all marched up the road to look at the hoof prints.

They were there all right. Lots of them. All over the muddy earth. Emma bent down and pressed her hand into one of the hoof marks. She stretched out her fingers wide.

"These can't be Sheltie's hoof prints," said Emma. "They're much too big. Sheltie has only little hoofs."

The grown-ups stood and stared. Emma was right. The hoof prints were far too big to be Sheltie's.

"Bahh!" said Mr. Crock. "Just keep that pony away, that's all." And he stomped off into his cottage.

That evening, Emma said good night to Sheltie and went to bed.

Sheltie stood with his fuzzy chin over the wooden fence. The little pony watched the moon come up over the roof of the house. And as it grew dark, he watched the stars come out one by one.

When the last light shining from the house went out, Sheltie trotted into his stable. He stood looking out into the paddock.

Sheltie was wide awake.

In the darkness of the shadows, Sheltie saw someone walking along. His ears pricked up as he watched a strange figure pass by the house and continue down the road.

Sheltie gave a blow and shook his mane.

He trotted over to the far end of the paddock for a better look. His keen eyes peered into the darkness, watching the dark figure disappear down the road and into the night.

☆ Chapter Six

The next day, when Mr. Crock went into his vegetable garden to count the cabbages, he found another two had gone missing.

"All right. That does it!" said Mr. Crock. And he went about setting a trap.

Mr. Crock tied a length of clothesline across the cabbage patch. He placed the line just above the ground and pulled it very tight. On the end of the line, Mr. Crock fastened three tin cans. Then he stood back with his hands on his hips and admired his work. He jiggled the line with his foot, and the tin cans rattled. Mr. Crock smiled. If anyone tried to walk through those cabbages now, he was going to know about it.

That night, Mr. Crock stayed awake. He sat in his shed, waiting. He waited until the moon came out and the sky grew dark. He waited and waited until everyone in Little Applewood was fast asleep.

Just after midnight, Mr. Crock heard a noise. He cocked his head to one side, and listened. The tin cans were rattling. There was someone in the vegetable garden!

Mr. Crock dashed out of the shed, waving a garden rake and shining a flashlight. But when he got to his cabbage patch, there was no one to be seen. Whoever it was had run away. Mr. Crock shined his flashlight along the rows of vegetables. Two more of his cabbages were gone!

Emma had been up for hours. It was another lovely, sunny morning. She filled Sheltie's water trough and gave him his pony mix. One small scoop, just like Mrs. Linney had said. And one tiny handful extra, for luck. That was Emma's idea.

Today, Sheltie and Emma were going to practice jumping. Emma could ride really well now. Most days, Emma rode Sheltie across Mr. Brown's field to Horseshoe Pond. There was a fallen log there that Emma was determined to jump one day. But first she had to practice.

The little jump Emma made in the paddock was six bricks high now. Emma set up the jump and placed the plank of wood across the bricks.

Sheltie was tacked up and eager to show off. He pranced around with a light, airy step lifting his feet high and blowing through his nostrils. His eyes twinkled as Emma mounted and settled herself in the saddle.

Mom came out of the house with little Joshua in her arms. Joshua loved to watch Emma and Sheltie riding around the paddock. One day, when he was big enough, Joshua was going to ride Sheltie, too.

Sheltie trotted around the paddock in a

wide circle, then approached the jump at a canter. Emma squeezed her heels. Up and over he flew, like a bird. Joshua clapped his hands.

"Good job, Emma!" called Mom. "Well done, Sheltie!"

Sheltie shook his mane and looked very pleased with himself. They turned around and took the jump again.

Then Sheltie jerked his head and nearly pulled the reins from Emma's hands. He stared across to the far end of the paddock and made funny snorting sounds. Emma glanced around to see what Sheltie was interested in. She saw Mr. Crock peeping over the fence.

Seeing Mr. Crock made Emma nervous. She rode Sheltie over to where Mom and Joshua were standing. Mom held out a carrot for Sheltie, but Sheltie was more interested in Mr. Crock.

Mom looked over to where Mr. Crock was standing and gave him a friendly wave. Mr. Crock turned sharply on his heels and stomped off back down the road.

"What a nasty man," said Emma. "Spying on us like that!"

"Don't take any notice, Emma," said Mom. "You just practice your jumping and make sure you lock the gate after you."

Emma patted the key hanging from the string around her neck. "I'll never forget, Mom. I promise."

Chapter Seven

When Mr. Crock arrived back in his garden, he set about making another trap. He made a wire snare and laid it carefully among the rows of cabbages. Then he hid the trap with a scattering of fallen leaves.

That night, Mr. Crock stayed up late again. He hid in his shed and waited.

The sun went down and the moon

came up. The night sky twinkled with stars and the shadows outside grew long and black.

Sheltie stood alone in the paddock with his chin resting on the wooden fence. He looked up the yard and watched the lights in the house go out, one by one.

Then Sheltie's ears pricked up. Someone was hurrying down the lane again, towards Mr. Crock's house. Sheltie swished his tail and trotted to the end of the paddock. He saw a man disappear down the dark, leafy road into the shadows.

Sheltie nudged at the top bar of the fence with his nose. The bar was loose and wobbled a little. Sheltie nudged it again. This time the bar creaked and moved a little more. Then Sheltie gave the bar a good hard push. The bar gave way and fell onto the grass.

The second bar was much lower. It couldn't have been more than six bricks high from the ground. Sheltie turned and moved a few steps away. Then he trotted forward and jumped clean over it.

Sheltie trotted down the dark road after the man. His long, shaggy mane flew behind him, shining silver in the moonlight.

Overhead, an owl hooted in the treetops, and Sheltie stopped in his tracks. He watched the man go through Mr. Crock's gate and into his vegetable garden. Sheltie followed and stood in the shadows of the apple trees. From his hiding place, Sheltie watched the man making marks in the earth with a funny stick. On the end of the stick was a horseshoe. Then the man bent down and pulled two cabbages clean out of the soil.

Sheltie shook his mane.

The man hollered as his foot became trapped in the wire snare. Sheltie heard the rattling of tin cans as Mr. Crock came rushing out of the potting shed. The thief freed his foot and ran away just before Mr. Crock arrived.

Mr. Crock shined his flashlight into the shadows. Sheltie stood frozen to the spot, caught in the beam of Mr. Crock's flashlight.

"Aha! Just as I thought!" shouted Mr. Crock. "Caught you red-handed." He walked up to Sheltie and grabbed a handful of the pony's mane in his fist. Sheltie didn't move. He stood there as quiet as a lamb as Mr. Crock tied him to a tree.

"Now then," said Mr. Crock. "Let's see what the police have got to say about this!"

The next morning, when Emma woke, she looked out through her little bedroom window and gasped. There was no sign of Sheltie anywhere. The paddock was empty!

Emma hurried downstairs just as the telephone rang. Mom answered the call. It was Officer Green. He said that Mr. Crock had caught Sheltie in his vegetable garden stealing his cabbages. Could they come as quickly as possible? Emma started to cry.

And Joshua, seeing his sister upset, began to cry, too.

Dad threw on his jacket and hurried down the road. Mom carried Joshua and held Emma's hand. They followed on behind.

Officer Green stood with Mr. Crock in the vegetable garden. Sheltie looked very

unhappy. He was still tied to the tree. When the little pony saw Emma he began to paw the ground. He shook his head and flicked his tail.

"Oh, poor Sheltie," cried Emma. She wanted to run to him. But Mom held on tightly to her hand. The tears ran from Emma's eyes in a great flood. Joshua sniffed and buried his head in Mom's shoulder.

"Mr. Crock here," Officer Green began in a very stern voice, "was disturbed last night by a noise in his garden. On investigating the noise, he caught your pony in the act of theft."

Emma's dad was standing among the remaining cabbages. Suddenly, Dad looked down and saw a long stick. On the end of the stick was fixed a horseshoe. He bent down to pick it up. Then he saw the snare. And caught in the wire hoop was an old boot!

"What's this?" said Dad. He held up the stick and the boot for everyone to see. "Looks like there was someone else here last night besides poor Sheltie."

Mr. Crock went very quiet. Officer Green took the stick and the boot to examine them. First, he studied the horseshoe

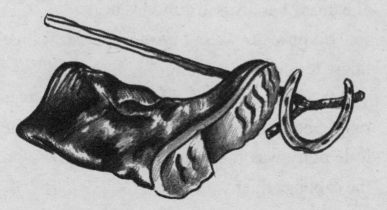

and matched them to the hoof prints in the soil. Then he studied the boot.

"Whoever lost this boot," said the policeman, "was using this stick to make hoof marks."

"And whoever did that," said Dad, "is the thief who has been stealing your cabbages, Mr. Crock."

"And trying to make it look like Sheltie," added Mom.

Emma broke free and ran over to Sheltie. She threw her arms around his neck.

"I knew it wasn't you, Sheltie. I just knew it."

Mr. Crock grunted. He knew Emma was right. Sheltie wasn't the thief after all. But the little pony was the only one who knew who the cabbage thief was.

Chapter Eight

Later that afternoon, Mrs. Linney came visiting. She said that everyone in Little Applewood was talking about Mr. Crock and his missing cabbages. Old Fred Berry had seemed very pleased at the news. He had told Mrs. Linney that perhaps now someone else would have a chance to win the special Cabbage Cup at the summer fair.

Fred Berry had been Mr. Crock's best friend until the day they'd had an argument. That was over ten years ago, and they hadn't spoken since. In fact, now they were the worst of enemies.

Emma was still very upset. Dad was in the paddock, fixing the rail back to the fence. Emma was in the paddock, too. She was giving Sheltie a good brushing. It wasn't much use though. Sheltie's coat was so thick and hairy. All the brushing in the world didn't seem to make any difference. But Emma liked to do it, and Sheltie enjoyed the attention. At least Emma managed to brush all the mud off Sheltie's legs.

The sun was shining now and all the clouds had disappeared.

When Emma saw Mrs. Linney coming

into the paddock, she smiled and gave a little wave. Mrs. Linney tried to cheer Emma up by talking about the summer fair.

"It's only a few days away now, Emma. It's a real treat. Everyone looks forward to it all year. There are stalls selling all sorts of things: homemade jam and cakes; pickles and canned fruit; old toys and knickknacks. There are raffles for prizes, and games and competitions. And there is a big tent where all the vegetables are judged to see who has grown the biggest and the best."

Emma made a face when Mrs. Linney mentioned vegetables.

"And there is a sheepdog trial," Mrs. Linney went on. "All the farmers bring their dogs and try to round up sheep into a little pen. And there's a refreshment stall selling sandwiches, tea, coffee, and soda. It's great fun, Emma. I bet you can hardly wait!"

Emma managed a weak smile.

"And don't forget Sheltie," said Mrs. Linney.

"Sheltie?" said Emma.

"Yes, Sheltie. Every year Sheltie gives rides to all the children. And you will be helping, won't you, Emma? You can lead Sheltie around the field. Sheltie loves it, don't you, Sheltie?"

Sheltie gave a nod and a loud blow. He remembered the peppermints he got every time he gave a ride. Sheltie became all frisky just thinking about it.

Emma said she would clean and polish Sheltie's tack. She was proud of Sheltie and wanted him to look his very best.

Emma bit her bottom lip. "Will Mr. Crock be there?" she asked.

"Oh yes. He wouldn't miss the summer fair for anything. He's won the Cabbage Cup every year. But don't you worry, Emma," said Mrs. Linney. "We'll all be there to keep Sheltie out of trouble."

No more cabbages went missing over the next few days. Mr. Crock had only six left, and he kept guard over them night and day. On the morning of the summer fair, he picked them all and laid them carefully in a huge cardboard box. They were the size of big basketballs.

Mom was busy making little cakes for the food stall. Dad was in the big field helping to put up the tent for the vegetable

show. And Emma was giving Sheltie one last brush. She was trying to comb all the knots out of his long mane. Sheltie just stood there as good as gold. He was looking forward to all those tasty peppermints.

At eleven o'clock, Dad came home for the cakes and took Joshua back with him to the fair. Mom followed later with Emma, leading Sheltie down the road and through Farmer Brown's meadow to the big field. An enormous white tent stood in the middle of the grass. Lots of little stalls were set up all around it.

Across the field was an area marked off with ropes. In the middle of it was a small wooden pen. Inside the pen were six woolly sheep. Sheltie liked the sheep. He wanted to go over right away to say hello. Emma had to keep hold of his reins to stop him wandering off.

One by one, the people started to arrive. Mrs. Linney was there, wearing a big straw hat. She carried a shoulder bag to keep the money that they would collect for Sheltie's rides. The summer fair was raising money to repair the town hall. Everything that was sold in the stalls would contribute toward a new roof.

Little Joshua was holding a big slice of chocolate cake. He stood there eating it with chocolate all around his mouth. He offered a piece to Emma, and she gave a little piece to Sheltie.

Sheltie liked chocolate cake. But he liked peppermints more. He knew that Emma had lots of peppermints in her pocket and kept nudging and pushing at her with his nose.

By twelve o'clock everyone in the town was there. Mr. Crock arrived with his box of cabbages. He carried them inside the big tent and laid them out on the wooden tables, ready for the judging. His cabbages really did look magnificent. They were much bigger than any of the others.

The prizes and the special Cabbage Cup

were displayed on a small table near the entrance. Mr. Crock looked at the shiny, silver Cabbage Cup and smiled to himself. The judging for the prized Cabbage Cup was the highlight of the summer fair. When he came out of the tent, Emma tried to hide herself behind Mrs. Linney.

"Good afternoon, Mr. Crock," said Mrs. Linney.

Mr. Crock touched his cap and grunted.

FRED BERRY

Sheltie pawed the ground and gave a loud snort.

When Fred Berry arrived with a handcart full of cabbages, Sheltie became very restless. He blew and snorted and swished his tail.

"Good afternoon, Fred," said Mrs. Linney.

Fred Berry smiled. "What a lovely day, Mrs. Linney!"

Then he gave Sheltie a funny look and pushed his handcart into the big tent.

One of Fred Berry's cabbages was gigantic. It was much bigger than all the others, and even bigger than any of Mr. Crock's. Fred laid it out carefully on the table with the others, next to a card with his name on it.

When he left the tent, Fred gave Emma a nice smile. Sheltie pawed at the grass with his hoof. Something was upsetting Sheltie, but Emma couldn't figure it out.

Chapter Nine

A little boy came up to Emma. He held fifty cents in his hand and asked Emma for a ride on Sheltie. Mrs. Linney took the money, put a riding hat on the boy, helped him up into the saddle.

Emma led Sheltie slowly around the big field. Sheltie behaved very well and walked at a steady pace. Emma was very proud of him. When the ride was over, Emma gave Sheltie a peppermint. Sheltie crushed it between his teeth with a loud crunch.

There were more children waiting for rides. Emma led them all around the field one after another.

"What a lovely pony," said all the moms and dads. They patted Sheltie and laughed as he gobbled the peppermints.

Little Joshua had a ride. His face beamed with a happy smile as he rode Sheltie around the field. Mom walked along next to him. Sheltie was extra careful and didn't bump or jog once. But when they passed Fred Berry, Sheltie's ears suddenly flattened and a funny look twinkled in his eyes.

When the time came for the judging of

the vegetables, everyone made their way into the big tent. Emma stayed outside with Sheltie and watched from the entrance.

The judging for the Cabbage Cup began. Emma listened to the announcement over the loudspeaker. "First prize and this year's Cabbage Cup go to Mr. Fred Berry!"

Emma jumped back as Mr. Crock stormed out of the tent.

"Bahh!" he said as he rushed past.

A big cheer came from inside the tent and Fred Berry appeared, holding the shiny Cabbage Cup above his head. Again, Sheltie's ears went back and a funny look appeared in his eyes.

What is wrong? thought Emma.

The next event was the sheepdog trial. The sheep were released from their little wooden pen. And one by one, the dogs tried to round up all six sheep and get them back in the pen within two minutes.

Each farmer gave directions to his dog with a series of whistles. It was funny to watch. Little Joshua jumped up and down and tried to whistle. All he could manage was to blow air.

The dogs worked very hard, running here and there, up and down. Sometimes the sheep stayed together in a tight bunch, and sometimes they all ran off in different directions. Most of the dogs managed to get two or three sheep into the pen. But no one was able to round up any more than that.

The last dog in the competition was Mr. Brown's black and white collie. He was very good and managed to get four sheep into the pen. Everyone cheered, and Mr. Brown was very pleased.

Then a strange thing happened. While Emma was busy watching the sheep, Sheltie suddenly lurched forward. His reins slipped through Emma's hands. Then

Sheltie ran off and trotted into the center of the field.

The sheep were out of the pen again and stood quietly munching the long grass. Sheltie went to work. All on his own, without any help from anyone, Sheltie trotted backwards and forwards rounding up the sheep one by one. Emma watched as Sheltie gathered all the sheep together into a tight bunch and drove them straight into the enclosure. All six sheep were safely inside the little pen!

The crowd cheered and clapped. Even Mr. Brown joined in. He waved his best cap in the air.

Mrs. Linney went to catch hold of Sheltie.

"Good boy, Sheltie, good boy." She reached forward for the reins. But Sheltie wasn't going to be caught. He was having far too much fun! His eyes twinkled and he shook his long mane. Then he was off again.

Sheltie trotted away in a straight line, across the field and into the big tent. There was a loud crash as the naughty pony knocked the trophy table over.

The next table held all the cabbages. Sheltie took Fred Berry's prizewinning cabbage in his teeth and ran out of the tent. Several hands tried to grab him, but Sheltie was too fast. Off he went, holding the cabbage up in front of him.

The cabbage was really huge. It was so big that Sheltie couldn't see properly. He ran straight through a line of little flags strung out across the field. The line snapped and all the flags became tangled around his neck.

Sheltie ran as fast as he could, trailing the line of flags behind him. He looked so funny that Emma started to laugh, even though Sheltie was being very naughty. Other people were laughing, too. Little

Joshua was jumping up and down and pulling Mom along. Officer Green and a whole crowd of people chased after Sheltie. But Sheltie didn't stop.

He ran right back across the field and out through the lower gate. The gate led on to a muddy path that wound its way up to the community gardens. The gardens were little plots of land laid out in neat, tidy rows, where some of the villagers grew vegetables.

The farmers' dogs barked and ran ahead of the crowd. Everyone followed to see what Sheltie was up to. When Sheltie got to the gardens, he raced over to the potting sheds. He stood in front of one and kicked the wooden door with his hoof.

Chapter Ten

Dad was the first to reach Sheltie. He pulled the line of flags free from the pony's neck. Sheltie dropped the giant cabbage at the shed door and let out a loud whinny. Emma had never heard Sheltie make such a noise before. When Officer Green and everyone else arrived Sheltie began to kick at the shed door again.

"That pony is a nuisance to everyone," said Mr. Crock. He had followed Sheltie like everyone else. "It ought to be locked away where it can't do any more damage!"

Sheltie began to kick at the door again.

"Stop it, Sheltie. Stop it at once," said Dad.

But Sheltie wouldn't stop. Emma tried to pull Sheltie away but he wouldn't budge.

"There must be something in there," said Mrs. Linney. She peered through a tiny crack in the wooden door.

"Who owns this shed?" asked Officer Green.

Fred Berry stepped forward, looking very guilty. He was holding the prized Cabbage Cup in his hands.

"I do," he said. "It's my garden shed."

"And what's in there that could be upsetting the pony?" asked the policeman. Sheltie was very quiet now.

"Only some old tools, flowerpots, and odds and ends," said Fred. Sheltie suddenly gave a loud whinny. Emma jumped back with a start.

"Would you mind unlocking the door, Mr. Berry? So that we can take a look inside."

Fred's face turned bright red.

"But there's nothing in there," he said. "Just a lot of old rubbish."

"Then you won't mind unlocking it, will you?"

Fred Berry had no choice. He took a key from his jacket pocket and unlocked the door.

Everyone was gathered around, wondering what could possibly be in the shed to make Sheltie behave so strangely. Officer Green went inside. Emma's dad followed.

"Well, well, well. What's all this?" said the policeman. Mr. Crock pushed his way through and stood by the open door. He looked inside.

"My cabbages!" said Mr. Crock. "My stolen cabbages! I'd know them anywhere." And there, sitting on a wooden bench at the back of the shed were seven enormous green cabbages. Mr. Crock's prize vegetables.

On the floor in front of the bench was one old boot. Officer Green bent down and picked it up. It was exactly the same as the old boot found in Mr. Crock's garden.

"And what have you got to say about all this, Mr. Berry?" said the policeman.

Poor old Fred owned up to the theft.

"All right," he said. "I admit it. I stole the cabbages."

"Thief!" snapped Mr. Crock. "Can't grow your own so you think you can steal mine."

"Do you have an explanation, Mr. Berry?" asked Officer Green. Fred Berry lowered his head in shame.

"I stole them because old Crock wins the Cabbage Cup every year," said Fred. "His cabbages are always bigger and better than anyone else's. I wanted to win. Just for once. I wanted to win the prize." He held the Cabbage Cup close to his chest.

Emma felt sorry for Fred. Although Emma knew that stealing was wrong, Fred didn't seem to be a bad man.

Mrs. Linney felt sorry for him, too. "I remember when you two used to be the very best of friends," she said. "All those years ago before your silly quarrel."

Mr. Crock remembered, too.

"What you did was wrong," said the policeman.

"I know. And I'm truly sorry for all the fuss and trouble I've caused," said Fred.

Suddenly, Emma spoke up. She was near to tears. "You're just two silly old men," she said. "What you should do is shake hands and be friends again."

Officer Green raised an eyebrow. "It may not be that simple, miss," he said. "After all, there has been a theft reported."

Mr. Crock stood there thinking. He didn't look so angry now. Emma thought he suddenly looked very sad.

"Bahh!" said Mr. Crock. He stepped forward and snatched the cabbage from the policeman's hands. "There's no need to arrest anyone," he said. "They're my cabbages. And if I don't mind Mr. Berry taking them, then there's been no crime committed."

The policeman looked puzzled.

"But you said they were stolen, Mr. Crock."

"I've changed my mind. I don't want anyone to get into trouble over something as silly as a cabbage. Let's just say they were missing, and now I've found them."

"Oh, thank you, Mr. Crock," said Emma.

Mr. Crock shook Fred Berry's hand. "Let's just forget this nasty business ever happened," he said. Mr. Crock gave Emma a smile. "And I'm sorry for blaming your clever pony for stealing my cabbages."

Sheltie tossed his head and snorted loudly.

"Well if you're sure, Mr. Crock," said the policeman, "then there's been no real harm done."

Fred Berry handed Mr. Crock the shiny Cabbage Cup. "I think this really belongs to you," said Fred. "After all it was your cabbage that won the prize."

Mr. Crock looked embarrassed.

"No, Fred," he said. "You keep it."

"I know," said Emma. "Why don't you two work together, and next year grow the biggest cabbages Little Applewood has ever seen!"

Everyone agreed.

"What a good idea. The perfect solution," said Dad. He was very proud of Emma. And everyone thought Sheltie was wonderful.

"Wasn't Sheltie clever?" said Emma. She gave him two peppermints as a special treat.

Mr. Crock was very happy to have his old friend back, and everything had worked out fine. They all walked back to the tent in the big field to have sandwiches, tea, and cake.

But when they got there, they found that

the sheep had eaten everything. All the sandwiches. All the cakes. And every single cabbage off the vegetable table! Everyone laughed, including Mr. Crock. It was the first time anybody had seen him laugh in years.

It had been a really exciting afternoon. And the best summer fair ever. Sheltie was awarded a blue ribbon for rounding up all

six sheep in the sheepdog trial.

Emma was so proud. She pinned the ribbon to Sheltie's bridle and stood next to him while Dad took a snapshot.

"Smile, Emma. Say cheese. And you too, Sheltie."

Sheltie tossed his head and gave a funny grin. He really was a very special pony.

Sheltie ACTIVITY FUN PAGES
Developed by Stasia Ward Kehoe

SHELTIE THE SHETLAND PONY QUESTIONS

1. What is Emma's little brother's name?
2. What is Sheltie's favorite treat?
3. What does Mr. Crock want to win at the summer fair?
4. Who was Mr. Crock's best friend?
5. How many sheep does Sheltie round up into the pen?
(answers below)

WALK, TROT, GALLOP

The way in which a horse uses its legs and feet to move forward is called a gait. There are three natural gaits: walk, trot, and gallop. The slowest speed is the walk. The trot is a faster. The gallop is a type of run. Pretend you are a pony. Try walking, then trotting, and then galloping around your backyard or a nearby park. Have a friend pretend to be a horse trainer and call out "Walk," "Trot," and "Gallop" as you and other "horses" prance around. Or make up a pranc-

Answers: 1. Joshua 2. Peppermints 3. The Cabbage Cup 4. Fred Barry 5. Six

90

ing pony dance by performing walking, trotting and galloping movements to some lively music.

A PONY FOR A PRESENT

Emma is surprised and thrilled when she realizes that Sheltie will be her very own pony. Imagine how you would feel if you were given a little horse as a gift. Write a short story called "A Pony for a Present" in which the main character gets a pony. Be sure to include the name of the pony, how the character receives the pony, and how he or she feels about receiving it. Draw a picture of a pony to illustrate your story.

HORSE ART

Turn your favorite animal into a work of art with this fun collage craft. You will need:

- A sheet of white paper
- A slightly larger sheet of colored paper
- Safety scissors
- A glue stick
- Old magazines (Hint: Ask an adult to help you find these.)

Look through the magazines to find pictures of horses.

Cut out the pictures and glue them onto the white paper. Make sure the edges of the pictures overlap so that no white paper is showing. When the white paper is completely covered with great horse pictures, glue it onto the colored paper to create a frame. Your collage is ready to hang!

HORSE BREED SCRAMBLE

Can you unscramble the names of these horse breeds? (answers below)

1. NIBAAAR
2. APOSOALAP
3. EGINBLA
4. CDEDSAYLEL
5. GROMAN
6. UTSNAGM
7. LAMOONIP
8. SOKLFUF

Answers: 1. Arabian 2. Appaloosa 3. Belgian 4. Clydesdale 5. Morgan 6. Mustang 7. Palomino 8. Suffolk

PONY POINTERS: HORSE BREEDS

For hundreds of years, breeders have worked to develop different types of horses to suit all sorts of human needs from transportation to farming. Horse breeds can be divided into three groups: heavy (or draft) horses, light horses, and ponies. A pony is a breed of horse that stands no more than 56.8 inches high at the shoulder. Shetland ponies are some of the world's smallest ponies.

Everyone needs Kitten Friends!

Fluffy and fun, purry and huggable, what could be more perfect than a kitten?

written and illustrated by

Jenny Dale

#1 Felix the Fluffy Kitten
0-689-84108-6 $3.99

#2 Bob the Bouncy Kitten
0-689-84109-4 $3.99

#3 Star the Snowy Kitten
0-689-84110-8 $3.99

#4 Nell the Naughty Kitten
0-689-84029-2 $3.99

#5 Leo the Lucky Kitten
0-689-84030-6 $3.99

#6 Patch the Perfect Kitten
0-689-84031-4 $3.99

ALADDIN PAPERBACKS
Simon & Schuster Children's Publishing
www.SimonSaysKids.com